GAVIN CENTRAL SCHOOL
DISTRICT 37
INGLESIDE, ILLINOIS

READING IMPROVEMENT GRANT

The Great Green Turkey Creek MonSter

Story and Pictures by
JAMES FLORA

A MARGARET K. McELDERRY BOOK
ATHENEUM
NEW YORK

FOR MAIFY JENSEN
FROM UNCLE JIM

Atheneum
Macmillan Publishing Company
866 Third Avenue, New York, NY 10022
Collier Macmillan Canada, Inc.
Printed in the United States of America
First Edition
7 9 11 13 15 17 19 20 18 16 14 12 10 8

Library of Congress Cataloging in Publication Data
Flora, James. The great green Turkey Creek monster.
"A Margaret K. McElderry book."
[1. Humorous stories] I. Title.
PZ 7.F663Gt [Fic] 75-43894
ISBN 0-689-50060-2

t all began early last Tuesday morning.

The town of Turkey Creek was beginning to wake up.

The sun had just opened one eye and blinked the other when Sheriff Billy Burton walked down Main Street.

SMASH! TINKLE! CLINK!

A window broke in Bogwater's Shovel and Seed Store.

The Sheriff yanked out his gun and shouted, "COME OUT WITH YOUR HANDS UP!"

Nobody came out.

With a crash another window broke. A big, green arm reached out and snatched the Sheriff's gun.

The Sheriff ran to a telephone and called his deputy.

"Get the police and the fire department and hurry down to the Shovel and Seed Store," he yelled into the phone. "The place is crawling with great, green monsters. I need help."

When he got back to the seed store the monsters' arms were creeping out of the windows and wiggling out of the chimney.

As he got closer, the Sheriff was goggle-eyed to see that the arms had leaves. He didn't know any kind of animal that had leaves. It had to be something else.

It had to be some sort of monstrous vine.

With a great whine of sirens and flashing lights the police and firemen pulled up to the seed store.

The firemen took axes and tried to chop the thing to pieces, but it snatched the axes from their hands.

They turned firehoses on it, but it just drank the water and grew faster than ever.

They tried to saw it. They even tried to freeze
it with chunks of ice, but nothing seemed to stop
it. It grew faster and faster.

The Sheriff howled to one of his deputies,
"Fetch Ernie Bogwater. It's his store. He'll know
how to stop this crazy whatcha-ma-callit."

Ernie Bogwater took one look at his store full of creepy crawlers and said, "Good grief! It's a Great Green Hooligan Vine. Somebody must have sent me the wrong kind of seed."

"I don't care what it is," yelped the Sheriff. "I want you to stop it."

"I can't," said Ernie Bogwater. "There is just no way to stop a Hooligan Vine. Once they start growing they never stop until they decide they are big enough. Then they stop. It generally takes about six days."

"SIX DAYS!" screeched the Sheriff. "We can't wait six days. It has already tied up the fire truck and grabbed all of the axes and fire extinguishers. Now it's coming for us. *Run for your life.*"

The Hooligan Vine grew so fast that you had to run to keep ahead of it. If you walked it would soon catch up, and when it did it was likely either to tickle you until you cried "Uncle" or dump ice cream down your collar.

It wasn't a mean vine or a nasty vine, but you never knew what it was going to do next.

It climbed the church steeple and rang the bell and woke up all of the bats and birds.

It opened fireplugs and gave itself a shower.

It picked up John Schwartz's new bicycle and put glue on the seat. Poor John Schwartz had to ride around for three days before he could get off.

It went into the Turkey Creek Clothing Store and came out wearing red underwear and polka dot neckties.

Mrs. Emma T. Grogan was taking a nice hot bath in her bathroom. The Hooligan Vine opened a window and dropped a live skunk into the tub with her.

When it came to the school, the Hooligan Vine stopped. It opened a window and crawled inside.

The children were afraid and began to howl and blubber, but the big vine didn't hurt them. It hugged all of the girls and patted the boys on the head.

It liked children.

It looked into all of their lunch boxes but it didn't eat anything. Not even a banana or an apple.

It went into the coatroom and tied knots in the teacher's coat sleeves.

It tickled Miss Ella Spooner, the first grade teacher. She laughed so hard her glasses fell into the wastebasket.

It wrote I LOVE MISS SPOONER on all of the blackboards.

It locked the principal in the girl's room *and he isn't a girl.*

The principal was so mad that he closed the school for the rest of the day. The children got to go home early.

A lot of them got on the vine and rode it down the street like a horse.

The vine didn't mind. It liked it.

When a little girl fell off, the vine picked her up and put her back on again.

TURKEY
CREEK
PAINT
STORE

By eleven o'clock in the morning most of the buildings in town were jammed full of Hooligan Vine.

The vine went into the Turkey Creek Paint Store and fetched out paint and brushes. It painted almost every house with stripes, zig-zags, stars and blotches.

It was something to see.

It painted zebra stripes on Maify Jensen's cow.

The cow liked it.

It painted HA-HA all over the jail house.

The Chief of Police didn't like that.

It hauled a lot of blueberry pies out of Bingcherry's Bakery and stuffed them into people's mailboxes. Every kid in town thought it was the best mail he had ever gotten.

It bammed through the Turkey Creek Molasses Factory and dumped seven barrels of molasses in Franklin Heller's swimming pool.

Franklin Heller was swimming when it happened.

It pushed the garbage truck inside the movie theater. Everybody came running out and said, "Hoo boy! What a stinky picture."

TURKEY CREEK MOLASSES CO.

STAR

NOW SHOWING
THE PERFUMED GARDEN

The Sheriff didn't know what to do so he called the Governor.

"Governor, we've got a Great Green Hooligan Vine that's turning Turkey Creek upside down. Can you send the National Guard or the Army to help us get rid of it?"

"I'll be right over in my helicopter and pick you up," said the Governor. "We'll look and see how bad it is."

In no time at all they were buzzing over Turkey Creek in the Governor's helicopter.

"Say, this is something. I've never seen anything like it in my whole life," the Governor said. "The school bus is stuck in the candy factory. The fire engine is on top of the hardware store and the railroad track runs into the river.

All of the houses are so full of creepers that nobody can go home to change his socks or look at TV. It's terrible."

"Every house except that one." The Sheriff pointed. "There aren't any vines near it. I wonder why?"

"Let's fly down and see," said the Governor. "Maybe someone who lives there has found a way to fight the Hooligan Vine."

The helicopter landed in front of the house.

They saw a boy sitting on the front steps.

He was playing a trombone.

"Every house in town is full of Hooligan Vine except yours," said the Governor. "How do you keep it out?"

"I play my trombone when it gets near," said the boy. "I don't think it likes trombone music. Watch this."

The boy walked across the yard to where the vine lay waiting. He played "Bobby Shaftoe" on his trombone.

The vine shivered and crept back several feet.

The boy played louder.

The vine shuddered and clapped leaves over its ears.

"That's the secret!" shouted the Governor. "The Hooligan Vine has trombonitis. Now we know how to lick it. You will get a medal for this boy. What's your name?"

"Argie Bargle, sir," said the boy.

"Well, Argie Bargle, you have just earned a place in history," said the Governor. "Keep playing your trombone while I make a call on my radio."

"*Mayday! Mayday!*" the Governor shouted into his radio. "We've got big trouble in Turkey Creek. I want every trombone player in the state to come here as fast as he can."

"They had better hurry," said the Sheriff. "The vine has started to creep in again."

"That's because the boy has stopped playing," said the Governor. "Play, boy, play."

"I can't," said Argie Bargle. "I've been playing so long that my lip got tired and won't work anymore.

He tried to blow into the trombone but all that came out was a tired *blurp*.

The Sheriff grabbed the trombone and tried to play; but all he could make was a thin little *bleep*.

In a flash the vine grabbed the trombone and tied it into a knot.

"QUICK! INTO THE HELICOPTER!" the Governor cried.

But they were too late. Before they could start the engine, the Hooligan Vine tied knots in the rotor blades.

"*Run for the house*," Argie Bargle shouted. "*I've got some trombone records inside.*"

Once again they were too late. The vine had crawled through the windows and was rocking in the chairs and poking around in the refrigerator.

The Sheriff pulled Argie Bargle and the Governor into the cellar and slammed and locked the door.

"*Whew!* That was a close shave," said the Governor, wiping his brow.

Over their heads they could hear the Hooligan Vine playing the piano and running water in the sink.

The oven door opened and closed.

"It's baking a cake," said Argie Bargle.

Suddenly there was a noise at the door. The knob turned.

HOME SWEET
HOME

"It's trying to get in here!" said the Sheriff. "Quick. Let's nail some boards over the door."

They dashed around looking for boards and nails.

"SHHH-H! QUIET! LISTEN!" the Governor shushed them.

The noise at the door had stopped.

So had the rocking chairs and the piano.

Faintly, far in the distance, they could hear the sound of trombones. They grew louder and louder.

"Thank goodness. They've come in time." The Governor opened the door and peeked out.

The Hooligan Vine had gone.

They rushed out of the cellar and met a great parade of trombone players marching down the street.

The Governor, the Sheriff and Argie Bargle cheered and marched along behind them.

Ahead they could see the vine pulling out of houses and cars and racing backward down the street. The trombone players were pushing it back toward Bogwater's Shovel and Seed Store.

Back and back it went, swishing and wiggling, until it disappeared into the seed store.

The trombone players marched after it, right into the seed store, playing louder and louder.

The Great Green Hooligan Vine became smaller and smaller until it had slithered back into the box where it had started in the morning.

COW LANE

The Sheriff clapped a lid on the box and tied it good and tight with baling wire.

"Now I'll burn it," he said. Then it will be gone for good and never come back."

All of the children began to cry.

"Please don't burn it, Mr. Sheriff," they begged. "It was such a good vine. It didn't hurt us. It hugged and patted us and let us ride on its back. It didn't even eat anything out of our lunch boxes. Please save it for the Fourth of July. Then we can ride on it again."

"Well! I don't know about that," said the Sheriff. "What do you think, Governor?"

"I don't mind," said the Governor. "But when you let it loose, you've got to have plenty of trombone players around so you can toot it back into the box again."

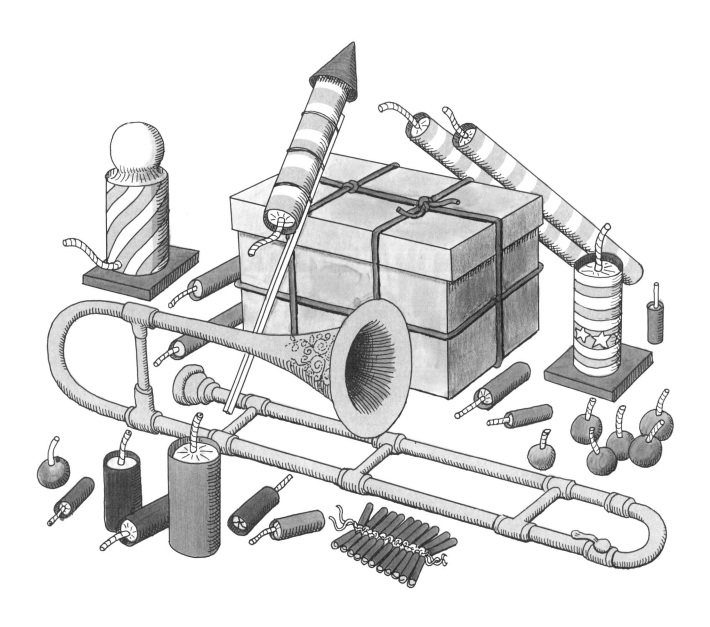

So that's the way things stand.

The town of Turkey Creek is going to let the Great Green Hooligan Vine out of its box next Fourth of July.

It's going to be a grand celebration.

You are invited, if you want to come.

You know where Turkey Creek is, don't you?

Well, you go past Indianapolis about three miles and then turn left. It's the first road after you pass Alabama.

And don't forget to bring your trombone.